Are you a child who's **"good as gold"**?
Do you do everything you're told?

For if you are then I'm afraid . . .

. . . A terrible mistake's been made!

I know you're only on page two
(And I'm sorry if you bought it new)

But this is **NOT** the book for you.
Please close it.

NEVER GROW UP

...EF AND MAGIC OF

ROALD DAHL

Illustrated by Quentin Blake

PUFFIN

In the days when I was illustrating his books, I came to know Roald Dahl well, and so I have a sense of how much he must have enjoyed inventing the phrase "never grow up, always down". Of course, first of all it's a joke with words, but it means more than that – even if you get bigger and more important, you still have to keep lively and imaginative. That is what this book is about, and I am sure it's just the sort of thing that Roald would have approved of. I hope he would have liked the drawings too.

PUFFIN BOOKS

UK|USA|Canada|Ireland|Australia|India|New Zealand|South Africa

Puffin Books is part of the Penguin Random House group of companies whose addresses can be found at global.penguinrandomhouse.com

First published 2021

This edition published 2022

Written by Al Blyth and Stella Gurney

Text copyright © The Roald Dahl Story Company Ltd, 2021

Illustrations copyright © Quentin Blake, 2021

ROALD DAHL is a registered trademark of The Roald Dahl Story Company Ltd   www.roalddahl.com

A CIP catalogue record for this book is available from the British Library

Printed and bound in China   001

The authorized representative in the EEA is Penguin Random House Ireland, Morrison Chambers, 32 Nassau Street, Dublin D02 YH68

ISBN: 978–0–241–41942–7

All correspondence to: Puffin Books, Penguin Random House Children's,

One Embassy Gardens, 8 Viaduct Gardens, London SW11 7BW

MIX
Paper from
responsible sources
FSC® C018179

Right now!

Go on!

SHOO!!

But look!
YOUR sticky little paw
Turned directly to page four,
Which leads me to suspect you're *not*
A pure angelic type of tot.

No.

YOU'RE a more unusual child,
The kind who's **mischievous** and **wild**.

Who eats too many **sweets**,
and then . . .

Throws most of them back up again!

Brushes their teeth
with **superglue** . . .

Then has to pull out one or two!

Paints their tongue . . .

And scrapes their knees . . .

Then fills their underpants with bees!

The kind who climbs a prickly pine
But falls

CRASH!

onto a
porcupine!

(Then has to bend down while their mum
Removes the prickles from their bum.)

I'm sure some grown-ups find your antics
Send them absolutely frantic,

Until they point and shout and frown . . .

"Hey!"

"STOP THAT!"

"Drop that!"

"Put that down!"

"Don't pick your nose!"

"DON'T trick
your mother!"

"DO NOT
SMEAR YOGHURT
ON YOUR
BROTHER!"

But WHY do grown-ups get so mad
When we do things they think are bad?

Have they forgotten the sensation
Of glorious gunky gunge creation?

Adding some of this

A dash of that

To make . . .

a
slimy,
snot-green
SSSPLAT!

Perhaps each year grown-ups grow old
Makes them ninety times less bold . . .

. . . Until their lives are spent pursuing
The boring things they're used to doing.
And they forget to stop and see
Just how **exciting** life can be –
Filled with adventure, hidden **magic**!

It's simply, absolutely tragic
To watch them waste each day (and weekend!)

Until they die.

That's it.
The End.

BUT . . .

It doesn't have to be this way!
Listen carefully to what I say:
There's a **secret**
that you might not know
About what happens
when you gr**OW** . . .

. . . Some people grow to ten feet T**ALL**
Without growing up at all!

Just look at all the very smartest
Scientists and famous artists
Who had the wit, the grit, the spunk
To think thoughts up-till-then unthunk.

Ignored the signs that said "NO WAY"
And went and did it anyway.

...It was once a crazy notion

To DIVE for miles

beneath

the ocean.

Till some spark had a bright idea
And invented scuba gear!

So pack a bag and go explore
The mountain tops of Ecuador!

Or build a jetpack,
   fly to **space**
To meet a
brand-new alien race!

Or be the first to find the lairs
   Of equatorial talking **bears**!

Or even cause a great sensation

By moving things with
concentration!

Or . . .

Be a wrestler!

Hair artiste!

Save the planet's rarest beast!

Whizz round in a helicopter,
A fearless, flying ostrich doctor!

Amaze the whole world when you bake . . .

THE
BIGGEST
EVER
CHOCOLATE
CAKE!!

One thing's for sure, it won't be easy.
Being bold is never breezy.
Sometimes you'll fall, sometimes you'll fail.
Just remember, when the grown-ups wail,
"THAT MAKES ME ABSOLUTELY FURIOUS"

The future's created by a curious,
Mischievous and disobedient few,
Who are (in fact) a lot . . . like . . .

...YOU!

So . . .

. . . Watch the world with glittering eyes,
Keep noticing where **magic** lies,
Question everything you're told,
Be outrageous! Break the mould!
Grow wise or silly, wide or tall,
Grow round in circles, big or small,

Dress all in rags or wear a crown
BUT . . .

... NEVER GROW UP,
always down!